# CALICO ILLUSTRATED CLASSICS

Alexandre Dumas's

# The **Three Musketeers**

ADAPTED BY: Jan Fields
ILLUSTRATED BY: Mike Lacey

magic
wagon

visit us at www.abdopublishing.com

Printed in the United States of America, Melrose Park, Illinois.
042010
092010
 This book contains at least 10% recycled materials.

Original text by Alexandre Dumas
Adapted by Jan Fields
Illustrated by Mike Lacey
Edited by Stephanie Hedlund and Rochelle Baltzer
Cover and interior design by Abbey Fitzgerald

**Library of Congress Cataloging-in-Publication Data**

Fields, Jan.
  Alexandre Dumas's The three musketeers / adapted by Jan Fields ;
illustrated by Mike Lacey.
    p. cm. -- (Calico illustrated classics)
  Summary: In seventeenth-century France, young d'Artagnan initially
quarrels with, then befriends, three musketeers and joins them in
trying to outwit the enemies of the king and queen.
  ISBN 978-1-60270-751-1
  1. France--History--Louis XIII, 1610-1643--Juvenile fiction. [1.
France--History--Louis XIII, 1610-1643--Fiction. 2. Adventure and
adventurers--Fiction.] I. Lacey, Mike, ill. II. Dumas, Alexandre, 1802-
1870. Trois mousquetaires. III. Title. IV. Title: Three musketeers.
  PZ7.F479177Al 2010
  [Fic]--dc22
                                                          2010002616

# Table of Contents

# D'Artagnan

The young man sat tall and proud on his yellow horse as he entered the town of Meung, France. His hand rested on the hilt of his sword and he kept a sharp eye out for anyone who might mock him or his horse.

The horse was a gift from his aging father. It was old and skinny and very yellow with a bald tail. The horse hung its head below its knees as it walked, as if constantly ready to stop and graze. The sight of the stiff young man and the tattered horse brought a few smiles, but no one dared offend the fierce young man.

The young man was headed from the Southern town of Gascony to Paris with hopes of joining the King's Musketeers. He carried a letter from his father, who had known the captain of the Musketeers when they were both young men. The letter urged Monsieur de Treville to help his son however he could.

As d'Artagnan climbed down from his skinny horse, he heard the clear sound of laughter. He looked around sharply and caught sight of three men. A tall, dark-haired nobleman looked directly at d'Artagnan's horse and said something to his friends. The man laughed rudely.

D'Artagnan stormed over to them. "Do you laugh at my horse?" he demanded.

The nobleman looked down his long nose at d'Artagnan, examining him from boots to beret. Finally he said, "I laugh little enough, but I will laugh when it suits me."

D'Artagnan drew his sword and shouted, "But it doesn't suit me!" The nobleman merely turned to walk back toward the inn. D'Artagnan dashed after him but was stopped when the nobleman's friends attacked him.

They walloped him with a shovel and a stick, until they had knocked him unconscious.

The innkeeper sent servants out to carry the young man inside. They placed d'Artagnan on a bed and wrapped a ragged bandage around his head. Then the innkeeper hurried to the nobleman's side. "Are you safe and sound, Excellency?" he asked.

"Perfectly," the man said. "Seeing a hothead bashed about does me little harm. Will he recover?"

"He will," the innkeeper said. "He even rallied enough to call out challenges to you. We went through his things. He has enough money to stay in our care for a bit and he carries a letter for Monsieur de Treville."

The nobleman looked at the innkeeper sharply. "Are you sure?"

"Oh yes," the man said. "The letter is tucked in his cloak in the pile of his things in the kitchen."

"Thank you," the nobleman said. "Please get my horse."

And so the nobleman prepared to leave after a quick visit to the inn's kitchen. D'Artagnan rallied enough to stagger to a window, intending to demand the nobleman meet him in a duel.

He saw the nobleman on his horse talking to a beautiful woman in a carriage. D'Artagnan was so distracted by the young woman that he forgot everything else. He leaned far out the window for a better look and was able to hear a bit of their conversation.

"Go to England, Milady," the nobleman ordered. "Notify his Eminence immediately if the Duke of Buckingham leaves London."

"Is that all?" the woman asked.

The nobleman passed her a box. "There are other instructions in here. Do not open it until you've crossed the channel. Now go!"

"And you?" she asked.

"Paris," he said. Then he turned his horse and galloped down the road with the woman's coach quickly leaving in the opposite direction.

"Paris," d'Artagnan said as he sank to the floor. "I will find you in Paris."

D'Artagnan's wound healed quickly but his temperament improved little. He found his letter missing and rushed around the inn yelling and flashing his sword.

"Oh, Monsieur," the innkeeper moaned, shaking. "The letter was surely taken by the man you challenged. He seemed very upset when he heard about Monsieur de Treville."

"Then he is a thief and I will find him in Paris," d'Artagnan said, mounting his yellow horse and riding away.

Just outside Paris, d'Artagnan sold his horse and entered Paris on foot, intent on seeking out Monsieur de Treville.

# The Audience

Many years before, Monsieur de Treville had arrived in Paris from Gascony. He had great plans and little money, much like d'Artagnan. Treville was poor but he was brave and smart and had become a friend and adviser of the king of France.

The king's most trusted adviser was Cardinal Richelieu. His power made him a dangerous rival for the king. So the king and the cardinal looked for ways to best the other. Each man secretly encouraged fighting between their personal guards.

The king placed Treville in charge of the King's Musketeers and stressed the importance of loyalty and skill in these guards. The

Musketeers were loud, impulsive, and joyfully violent. It was into this group of rowdies that d'Artagnan stepped as he entered the courtyard of Treville's house.

D'Artagnan stared around him wide eyed. He watched dueling games and heard endless bragging. He was especially surprised at the rude way the Musketeers talked about the cardinal. D'Artagnan's family admired both the king and the cardinal.

D'Artagnan was relieved when he was finally called to Treville's quarters. The older man greeted d'Artagnan politely.

"Would you wait just a moment while I deal with some others?" Treville asked.

"Of course," d'Artagnan answered with a slight bow.

The captain of the Musketeers walked to the door and called out, "Athos! Porthos! Aramis!"

Two of the Musketeers d'Artagnan had seen outside stepped in and stood with dignity. "The cardinal has complained of you to the king,"

Treville said. "He said you were caught behaving badly at an inn and the Cardinal's Guards were forced to arrest you." Then the captain scowled and looked around. "Where is Athos?"

"Sick," Porthos boomed. "I think it is smallpox."

"At his age? More likely he was wounded before the three of you ran like rabbits."

"Run? We did not," Aramis said. "They attacked us and wounded Athos, but we fought and escaped!"

Just then, a pale, shaky man strode in. "You called for me?"

"I did, but it seems I was misinformed. The King's Musketeers are the bravest men in the world," Treville said. At that Athos collapsed. Treville called for a doctor as Porthos and Aramis carried their friend from the room.

Finally quiet settled on the room again. Treville offered to send d'Artagnan to a fine regiment to train for a place in the Musketeers.

"But I am ready now," d'Artagnan insisted. "And you would know it if that wretched man had not stolen my letter for you." D'Artagnan described his near duel and later robbery by the hawk-nosed nobleman. "I will deal him yet for his stealing."

Treville looked at d'Artagnan thoughtfully. "Was he pale with dark hair and a scar here?" Treville asked, touching his temple.

"You know him!" d'Artagnan exclaimed. "Where can I find him?"

"Stay away from him," Treville warned. "He is a dangerous man."

"So am I," the young man muttered.

Treville shook his head in grim amusement as he wrote a letter of recommendation for d'Artagnan to become a cadet. The young man stood gazing glumly out the window as he waited. Just as Treville finished, d'Artagnan bolted from the room, yelling, "He won't get away this time!"

# The King's Musketeers

D'Artagnan raced toward the stairs in a blind rage. A Musketeer stepped out on the landing from another door and d'Artagnan slammed into him. His head struck the taller man's shoulder. The Musketeer cried out in pain.

"Excuse me," d'Artagnan muttered, recognizing the Musketeer as Athos.

A hand seized d'Artagnan's sash and pulled him to a stop. "I do not excuse you," Athos said. "Did you suppose that you may treat us rudely because you witnessed our scolding by Monsieur de Treville?"

"You give me a lesson in manners?" d'Artagnan asked, his pride pricked by the Musketeer's sharp voice.

"You could use one," the tall, pale man said. "Perhaps at noon, near the Carmes-Deschaux monastery?"

"I'll be there," d'Artagnan said, agreeing to the duel. Then the young man turned and raced down the stairs. He knew there was little chance of catching the stranger on the street but he couldn't give up.

At the bottom of the stairs, a group of Musketeers stood talking and posing. Porthos stood among them, showing off his handsome cloak and bright gold sash. Just as d'Artagnan passed, the wind caught the Musketeer's cloak and blew it against d'Artagnan. Porthos jerked his cloak back, managing to tangle up the younger man in the process.

D'Artagnan found himself jerked forward, his nose pressed against the back of Porthos's gold sash. D'Artagnan noticed it had an ordinary leather backing.

*No wonder he watches over his cloak so much,* d'Artagnan thought.

"Can you not see?" Porthos demanded, pulling the young man from his cloak.

"I see better than anyone," d'Artagnan said with a smile. "I can see why you don't like to turn your back on anyone."

D'Artagnan thought his remarks about Porthos's sash were quite witty, but the tall man flew into a rage. Before d'Artagnan realized what had happened, he was agreeing to his second duel set an hour after his first.

Again, the young man rushed out of the courtyard, but the stranger was definitely gone. D'Artagnan slumped with disappointment and turned back toward the courtyard. He saw Aramis speaking with several men. A delicate handkerchief was trapped under the Musketeer's boot.

D'Artagnan was certain the Musketeer would not want to lose such a lovely piece of linen, so he bent to tug the handkerchief free. He noticed Aramis stood on it very hard.

Finally, after a bit of a wrestle, d'Artagnan held it up.

"You dropped this?" he asked.

"I did not!" Aramis insisted as the other men howled with laughter. A lively bit of teasing followed as the men questioned why Aramis had such a delicate lady's handkerchief. "You all know I am only a Musketeer until I enter the priesthood," Aramis insisted. "What business would I have with a lady's linen?"

When the group finally broke up, Aramis turned on d'Artagnan. "Why did you try to humiliate me, sir?" he demanded.

"I did not," d'Artagnan said. "I thought it was your handkerchief."

"Then you are an idiot!"

D'Artagnan's temper soared and quickly another duel was arranged. Finally the young man walked down the street, glumly looking for the Carmen-Deschaux monastery.

"Oh well," he muttered. "If I am to be killed three times today, at least it will be by Musketeers!"

D'Artagnan arrived to find Athos waiting for him. The Musketeer still looked pale, and d'Artagnan felt bad about running into him earlier. He greeted the Musketeer politely.

"I am waiting for two friends to act as my seconds," Athos said.

"I am new to Paris and have no seconds," d'Artagnan said. "But I am honored to duel with a man as brave as you." The young man waited a moment. "My mother gave me a recipe for a salve with great healing power. I would be honored to share it with you."

The Musketeer smiled. "You have a good heart. If one of us does not die today, I believe we will be friends."

At this point, both men spotted Aramis and Porthos approaching. "My seconds!" Athos said.

"They are?" d'Artagnan said. "They are also here to duel with me, though not until after you."

Athos laughed. "You have been busy."

D'Artagnan said, "You are all here for a duel and I do not back down. But I apologize if I do not live to duel all of you. And now, on guard!"

The men drew their swords just as they heard voices calling them to stop. It was a small group of the Cardinal's Guards. Dueling was illegal in Paris and the guards were delighted to catch Musketeers in the act.

"We will have to fight them for the honor of our captain," Athos said quietly. "And there are five of them against three."

"Count yourselves not three but four," d'Artagnan said. "I will proudly fight with you."

And with that the Musketeers and the guards clashed swords. The fighting was furious. D'Artagnan was amazed to see the skill that Athos showed even though he was already badly wounded. D'Artagnan fought furiously at their side, and soon they had defeated the entire group of guards.

The Musketeers walked arm in arm with d'Artagnan, taking up the whole width of the street as they strutted back to Monsieur de Treville's house. They knew it was important to report this battle before the guards could tell their own story.

D'Artagnan was almost dizzy with happiness. He was not yet a Musketeer, but he finally felt on his way to becoming one.

# A Court Intrigue

When news of the Musketeers' victory spread, Monsieur de Treville scolded the group publically for endangering themselves. But he was delighted to share the news privately with the king. The king loved having something new to brag to the cardinal about.

The king was equally impressed by d'Artagnan's brave help. He rewarded the young man lavishly, and d'Artagnan shared his new wealth with his friends. He also rented pleasant rooms for himself and hired a servant.

Life was good for the friends for weeks, but eventually the money ran out. They helped one another with food, but soon it became clear they needed a new source of wealth.

Then, one early evening, d'Artagnan heard a knock at his door. It was his landlord Monsieur Bonacieux.

"I hear you are a brave young man," the landlord said. "My dear wife has been abducted. And since you owe me a small bit of back rent, I thought perhaps you would be willing to help."

"Tell me how this abduction occurred," d'Artagnan urged.

"My wife is the queen's linen maid. She told me the queen is afraid, for the cardinal wants to ruin her. I believe the cardinal has taken my wife in hopes of turning her into a spy," the landlord whispered.

"Was it the Cardinal's Guards who took her?" d'Artagnan asked.

"No," the landlord admitted. "It was a nobleman with dark hair, piercing eyes, and a scar on his temple. He sent a note threatening me if I try to rescue my wife."

"The scoundrel," d'Artagnan crowed. "Then your revenge will be mine as well."

"I can give you some money, if you are a bit short at the moment," the man said. "To help in the search." Suddenly the man stiffened and pointed out the open window. "It is the abductor!"

At that d'Artagnan dashed in pursuit, but the man slipped away again and all d'Artagnan found were Athos and Porthos heading his way. D'Artagnan quickly told them the story of the maid's abduction. When he got to the part about payment, his friends cheered.

"There's more to it than money," d'Artagnan scolded. "I'm concerned about the cardinal persecuting the queen."

"I've heard the queen has an English friend," Porthos said. "A man of power and wealth."

Athos nodded. "The Duke of Buckingham. I cheer their friendship if only to annoy the cardinal."

Just then, soldiers of the cardinal burst in downstairs and the friends heard Monsieur Bonacieux shrieking for help. The Musketeers rushed downstairs and the guards paused, expecting a fight. Instead, d'Artagnan merely said, "We are loyal to the king and the cardinal. Carry out your mission."

At the shocked look on the landlord's face, d'Artagnan whispered, "We must stay free to save you and your wife."

So the landlord nodded gloomily as he was led away.

# A Mousetrap

After Monsieur Bonacieux was arrested, the Cardinal's Guards turned the man's home into a trap. Everyone who knocked on the door was arrested and questioned.

D'Artagnan kept close watch over the comings and goings from his apartment. He even removed a section of his own floor so that he could hear any comments from the guards. And while d'Artagnan watched the house, his friends searched for clues all over Paris.

One day, d'Artagnan heard sounds of a struggle downstairs. He knew the trap had sprung on another visitor. As he listened, he realized it was the landlord's wife.

"We've been waiting for you," one guard said.

Quickly d'Artagnan sent his servant to fetch the Musketeers. Then the young man hurried downstairs to knock on the front door and put himself in the trap. He met the guards with his sword drawn. Soon four guards fled the house to escape the point of d'Artagnan's sword.

The young man turned to Madame Bonacieux. She was a lovely woman in her early twenties with dark hair and a charming smile.

"Where is my husband?" she asked.

"Held by the Cardinal's Guards," d'Artagnan said. "But not before he asked me to help you. How did you get away?"

"I tied my sheets together," she said, "and then I lowered myself from the window."

"Your husband believed you were kidnapped for political reasons," d'Artagnan said.

"I do believe he is right," she answered. "I know secrets that must not be shared."

"Then we must leave here before the guards return," d'Artagnan said. He took the young woman to Athos's home, for he knew she would be safe there while Athos was away. Madame Bonacieux gave him directions for sending a secret message to the palace so that someone could safely fetch her back.

After he followed the young woman's directions, d'Artagnan walked the streets of Paris. All he could do was dream of the beautiful young woman.

Soon, d'Artagnan found he had wandered near Aramis's house. He decided to talk to his friend about his mysterious day. He stopped suddenly when he spotted a cloaked woman tap at the closed window of Aramis's home. The window opened and another woman leaned out. The two exchanged handkerchiefs.

D'Artagnan crept closer as the cloaked woman turned away from the window. It was Madame Bonacieux! He hurried to her side and slipped an arm around her.

She struggled until he spoke and she recognized his voice. "Are you following me to keep me safe?" she asked with a smile.

"I would follow you anywhere," he said. "But why were you visiting Aramis?"

"I do not know anyone by that name and I cannot tell you who I was visiting. It is not my secret to tell."

"You are as mysterious as you are beautiful," d'Artagnan said. "But let me see you safely to your destination."

"We are here," she said as she stopped at a doorway. "Now you must go."

D'Artagnan hurried away but could not resist a peek back. He watched the door open and Madame Bonacieux slip through the narrow crack.

Then, he hurried home only to meet his servant in great upset. "Monsieur Athos has been arrested!" he cried.

"What? Why?"

"He came here and the guards assumed he was you," the servant explained. "They took him away."

"Oh no! I must tell them to release him at once!" d'Artagnan cried.

"No, master," the other man said. "Monsieur Athos said to tell you that you must remain free. He will give his real identity in three days."

D'Artagnan knew things were happening too quickly for him to sort out. He decided to talk to Monsieur Treville, but he soon learned the captain was not at home.

*Perhaps he has gone to see the king,* d'Artagnan thought. *I can watch for him and catch him upon his return.*

He hurried down the street, but as he neared his destination, he was stunned to see a Musketeer walking along with a woman in a cape.

"It is Madame Bonacieux and Aramis," d'Artagnan muttered. "And she said she knew him not."

He rushed to catch the couple, stepping in front of them to block their path. He looked full into the Musketeer's face.

"You're not Aramis," d'Artagnan said.

"I never claimed to be," the man said. "Step aside, please."

At that, the man drew his sword and d'Artagnan swiftly drew his own. Madame Bonacieux stepped between the swords and called out, "No, Your Grace."

"Your Grace?" D'Artagnan's sword dropped as he stared at the man. It was the queen's English friend, the Duke of Buckingham. "Forgive me and tell me how I can serve you."

"You are a brave man and I accept your service," the duke said. "Follow us and if you see anyone spying on us, kill them."

And so d'Artagnan followed them to the Louvre, but he had no opportunity to kill any spies that night.

Though d'Artagnan did not know it, the Queen Anne had just told the duke that they could never be more than friends. She gave the duke a token of her affection—a gold-inlaid rosewood box. Then she sent him away.

# Monsieur Bonacieux

While d'Artagnan was falling in love with his landlord's wife, the poor landlord sat in a dim cell deep within the Bastille. Accused of high treason, Bonacieux had spent days certain the guards would drag him away at any moment to be executed.

"But I have done nothing," he moaned. "Nothing at all." He nearly fainted from fright when he finally heard the tramping of boots approach his cell. The guards dragged the shaken man to the interrogation room.

"What treasonous plot have you hatched with your wife?" the magistrate asked.

"None," Bonacieux said. "If she has done such a thing, I renounce her and curse her!"

The magistrate waved away the man's words. "Then tell me of the plot between you and your tenant d'Artagnan."

"I only asked for his help," the landlord babbled. "I did not know it was wrong. I only wanted him to find my wife."

"And he did," the magistrate said. "He aided in her escape according to your plan!" The magistrate pounded a fist on the table, making the other man jump.

"My wife escaped?" the landlord said.

"Do not pretend to be innocent. We have d'Artagnan and he will confess. Guards!"

The guards brought in Athos.

"That's not Monsieur d'Artagnan," Bonacieux babbled. "He is too old. And Monsieur d'Artagnan is merely a soldier. This man is a member of the King's Musketeers. Look at his uniform."

The magistrate stared. "This is true. Why did you tell us you were d'Artagnan?" he demanded.

"I did not," Athos replied. "When I came to visit my young friend, your guards rushed at me and insisted I was d'Artagnan. I hated to argue with them, so I came along."

"Take them both back to their cells," the magistrate commanded.

"I would rather go home," Athos said mildly.

"To their cells!"

Now Bonacieux was certain they would hang him because of his foolish wife and that dratted young man. He slumped on the hard cot in his cell and waited to be called to the executioner.

Eventually the guards come for him. They shoved him into a carriage and drove away from the Bastille. "They are taking me to be hanged for sure," Bonacieux moaned.

When the carriage finally came to a stop, Bonacieux fainted and the guards dragged him to a small room, where a thin-faced man peered at him.

Again the terrified Bonacieux faced questions about his wife that he could not answer. He knew nothing of palace life, he insisted.

"Did you ever go anywhere with your wife?" the fierce-looking questioner asked. "Someplace she was secretive about."

"No, we went only to linen shops," the landlord answered. "I had no interest in linen so I waited outside always."

Just then, a servant slipped into the room. "Your Eminence," the man said. "The count is here."

Bonacieux trembled. *Your Eminence?* This could only be Cardinal Richelieu himself. "I'm going to die," he whimpered.

The servant opened the door to lead in a nobleman with a scarred face. "It's him!" Bonacieux shouted. "That is the man who abducted my wife!"

Both the cardinal and the count turned to look at him fiercely.

"No, it's not," Bonacieux then said. "I'm mistaken. Totally mistaken. I will never say such a thing again."

The cardinal ordered his servant to lead Bonacieux out. Then he turned to the count.

"The duke visited the queen last night."

"No," Cardinal Richelieu barked. "Don't tell me I missed another chance to catch them together."

"There is hope," the count said. "A lady's maid who is loyal to you reports the queen took a small rosewood box and gave it to the duke. Inside the box were diamond studs His Majesty had given her."

The cardinal smiled. "Then I must send a letter to milady. She will attend the next ball given by the duke. If the duke wears the queen's token, she can retrieve them for us."

The count nodded and slipped out of the room.

Bonacieux was brought back into the room. The frightened man could barely stand as the cardinal said, "I believe I am mistaken about you. You are loyal and brave and I have enjoyed our conversation. I wish to give you a gift to show my deep regrets at your ill treatment."

Bonacieux blinked in amazement. "A gift?"

"Yes." The cardinal handed over a bag filled with gold pieces. "I hope this will be enough to convince you to forgive me. I would love to have you visit again and perhaps chat about anything you might think would interest me."

"Oh yes, Your Eminence." Bonacieux bowed deeply and repeatedly as he backed out of the chamber. The cardinal only smiled as he watched his newest spy leave.

# The Plot Thickens

As soon as Monsieur de Treville heard that Athos was in prison, he hurried to speak to the king. He found the king talking with the cardinal.

"Ah, I've heard some outrageous things about your Musketeers," the king said.

"As have I," Treville said. "I have been told a brave and loyal Musketeer sits now in prison."

"He attacked my guards," the cardinal said. "And then he was found in a house of someone known to be plotting against the king."

"And when did this attack occur?" Treville asked.

"An hour earlier than his arrest," the cardinal said smoothly.

"Then it is a case of mistaken identity, for Athos spent most of the day with me and some of my guests," Treville said. "Then he went to visit his friend young d'Artagnan, whom you have met, Your Majesty. And that was when he was arrested."

"Ah, it would appear we need a trial that we may know the truth," the cardinal said.

"Perhaps," the king said, looking between the two men.

"You need a trial to know the truth?" Treville said. "My word is no longer proof? Then I must beg the king's pardon and resign at once as captain of the Musketeers. I had no idea I had lost the trust of the king." Treville bowed deeply as if ashamed.

"No, of course you have my trust," the king said, alarmed.

"Then you will release Athos?"

The cardinal broke in, clearing his throat. "Of course, we trust the word of Monsieur de Treville. You should pardon the Musketeer."

"Pardons are for criminals," Treville said. "Athos needs only to be released."

So the king arranged for the release of the Musketeer, but Treville left uneasy. Surely the cardinal was plotting something that could not end well for the king or the Musketeers.

And as soon as the captain of the Musketeers left, the cardinal turned to the king. He said, "The Duke of Buckingham has been in Paris. I believe he conspires against you."

"I should have had him arrested long ago," the king roared.

"But Buckingham is prime minister to the king of England," the cardinal said. "We must be careful how we proceed."

"Bah," the king huffed. "Sometimes I wonder if everyone isn't conspiring against me, you included."

The cardinal pretended to be offended. "I cannot believe the king doubts my loyalty. Perhaps you should speak with your queen. I have heard she corresponds with the duke."

The king swept out of the room in a fury and
stormed down the halls to visit the queen. She
sat crying in her darkened room. She knew the
king did not love her or trust her. The cardinal
had been her enemy ever since she had rejected
him as a suitor years before. She felt very alone.

When the king stormed into her chambers,
he demanded to see any letters she planned to
send. She mutely pulled one from the bodice
of her dress and handed it over. The king was

surprised to find it was to her brother and entirely about her fear of the cardinal.

The king was so delighted to find she was not writing love letters to the duke that he apologized. He announced he would have a grand ball for her even though he hated social gatherings himself.

"I know how much you like dancing, my dear," he told her.

"That's a grand idea," the cardinal said when he heard. "It will give her a chance to wear those diamonds you gave her. I doubt she's had the opportunity to show them off yet."

The cardinal trusted that milady would steal the diamonds and place them in his hands quickly. "Why not have the ball on the first of October?" the cardinal suggested.

When the king visited the queen, he told her of the date for the ball. "I would like you to come in full ceremonial dress," the king said. "And wear the diamond studs I gave you."

The queen turned very pale. "Of course," she said, barely whispering. "Could you tell me who suggested what I should wear?"

The king frowned. "The cardinal. Is there a problem?"

"No," the queen said. "I will do as you ask."

The queen had to get the diamonds back, but clearly someone had betrayed her. Whom could she trust? Her eyes fell on her linen maid, slipping in to put away dresses.

"Will you help me?" she asked.

"I would die for you, my queen," Madame Bonacieux said.

"I must get a message to the Duke of Buckingham," the queen whispered. "He must return the diamonds I gave him or I will be killed."

"Give me a letter," the maid said. "I will see it reaches him safely."

The maid rushed home, thinking at first of enlisting her husband's aid in the delivery of the letter, but she found Bonacieux much changed.

"You must have nothing more to do with these matters at court," he demanded. "The cardinal has opened my eyes to you."

"The cardinal!" she gasped.

"He shook my hand and called me his friend," her husband boasted, then he pulled the bag of coins from a cupboard and shook it. "He gave me a gift to show his friendship."

She knew then she could trust him with no part of the queen's secret. "You are right," she said. "You must surely know more about these things than me."

"Yes," he said, puffing himself up. "Now I must go on a small errand. I will be home soon." He slipped out the door and hurried off.

Almost the moment he left, Madame Bonacieux heard a knock at the door. It was d'Artagnan.

"Madame," he said, "allow me to say you have a wretched husband."

# The Journey

Madame Bonacieux looked at him with wide eyes. "You heard us?"

"Every word," d'Artagnan assured her. "I know the queen needs a brave, intelligent, and loyal man to go to London for her. As I have at least two of those qualities, I will go for her."

Madame Bonacieux sighed. "This is true. I have something that must be taken to London at once." She explained the mission and handed over the letter. "Now you know, and if you betray me, I will surely die."

"I would die first," d'Artagnan promised passionately.

"Then I have one more thing to give you," she said. "I am sure you will need it for the journey." She reached into the cupboard and pulled out the heavy bag of coins and passed them to d'Artagnan.

The young man laughed as he recognized the rattle of the bag. "The cardinal will fund this mission. That will make it all the better."

Suddenly the young woman hushed him. "My husband. He has returned."

D'Artagnan led her out through the side door and then upstairs to his room, where they knelt at the floorboards to listen.

"She's not here," Bonacieux said. "She must have gone back to the queen."

"You are a fool not to have questioned her more," a raspy voice answered. "Then the threat to the state would be eliminated."

D'Artagnan flinched. He recognized the voice immediately as the nobleman he had tried again and again to find.

"Don't worry," Bonacieux said soothingly. "My wife adores me and there is still time. She will tell me everything."

"Do it," the other man said. "And return straight to me."

When the downstairs door closed, Madame Bonacieux whispered, "The traitor! You must go at once and be very brave."

"I go for the queen," d'Artagnan said, then added, "and for you."

The young woman blushed as d'Artagnan left the house. He needed permission to leave Paris since he was a soldier. He knew no quicker way to get permission than to ask Monsieur de Treville. So he hurried to the man's home.

When he was led into Treville's study, he began to gush, "I have a secret mission from the queen that I must carry out."

"Has she given you permission to tell me about it?" Treville asked.

"No."

"Then keep your secret," the captain of the Musketeers said. "Only tell me how I can help."

D'Artagnan explained his need to leave Paris. Treville agreed to request a brief leave of absence for d'Artagnan so he could accompany Athos to a healing spring in England.

"I'll have Porthos and Aramis go as well," Treville said. "It will attract less attention for a group to go than for one man to try to make the journey alone. On a mission so important, the more of you who go, the more chance of it succeeding."

D'Artagnan agreed, grateful for the trust of the captain and for the company of his friends. The Musketeers were gathered quickly, along with their servants, and they left that night.

The journey was uneventful until the men made their first stop at an inn in Chantilly for some breakfast. They sat at a table with another traveler. The stranger made a few friendly remarks and breakfast passed quickly.

When the group rose to continue on, the stranger called out, "Will you share one last drink to the cardinal's health?"

"Of course," Porthos said cheerfully. "If you'll join me in a drink to the king as well."

"I know of no king except the cardinal," the man said.

"You, sir," Porthos said, "are drunk and should guard your tongue."

The man stood and drew his sword.

"You have been foolish," Athos said to his friend. "Deal with him quickly and join us. We ride!"

The three friends rushed to their horses and rode off. A few hours later, the friends were worried. Porthos should have rejoined them, but they could not turn back from this mission. They slowed a bit to give their friend a better chance to catch up.

Soon they came upon men working on the road. Aramis complained about the muddy work ruining his boots as they passed. To their alarm, the workmen ran to the ditch beside the road and took out muskets.

The first shot struck Aramis in the shoulder, but he galloped on for another two hours.

Finally Aramis called out weakly, "I am in no fit shape to go farther."

Athos and d'Artagnan practically carried their friend to the nearest inn, where they left a servant to care for him while they rode on.

"Perhaps Porthos will join you here," d'Artagnan said before they left.

The remaining men pushed their horses as hard as they dared. When the horses were beginning to stumble in the dark, they accepted that is was time to stop. They quickly found an inn.

The innkeeper was friendly and offered two rooms at opposite ends of the inn. "That won't work for us," d'Artagnan said.

"We will simply sleep down here," Athos said. "Mattresses are all we need."

The innkeeper tried to protest, but the men were fiercely insistent. One of the servants agreed to sleep in the stable with the horses. D'Artagnan's servant said he would take his place outside the door to the common room.

"That way, you won't be surprised in your sleep," he said. "That innkeeper was too friendly."

The night passed peacefully. In the morning, d'Artagnan and his servant hurried out to the barn to check on the horses while Athos went to settle the bill. He pulled out coins from the cardinal's stash and handed them over to the innkeeper.

"These are counterfeit," the innkeeper announced. "I shall have you all arrested!"

"You lying scoundrel!" The Musketeer pulled his sword. Immediately four armed men came from adjoining rooms and rushed at him.

"I'm trapped," Athos bellowed. "Ride, d'Artagnan, ride."

D'Artagnan and his servant heard Athos shout. They also spotted more men at the stables. Instead of fighting, d'Artagnan merely grabbed two beautiful horses tied up in front of the inn. He and his servant galloped away.

The mission was now up to him.

# Milady

"Could you see what happened to Athos?" d'Artagnan called to his servant, Planchet.

"Yes. He shot two men and was fencing with the others when we left."

"Brave as always," murmured d'Artagnan. He hated to leave his friends behind, but he knew the mission was everything. He and Planchet rode to Calais at such brutal speed that d'Artagnan's horse collapsed at the gate.

D'Artagnan and his servant left their horses at the gate and rushed to the docks. There, they heard a ship's captain talking to a dust-covered stranger. D'Artagnan stopped to listen.

"I could take you to England," the captain said. "But no ship can leave without permission from the cardinal."

"I have such permission," the dusty traveler said, holding up a packet of papers.

"Have it endorsed by the harbor master and we'll sail," the captain said.

As the man hurried away, d'Artagnan and Planchet followed. When they were out of sight of anyone, d'Artagnan said, "I must ask you to give me the packet of papers."

"I will not," the man said. "I am traveling in the service of the cardinal."

"And I am traveling in the service of the king and the queen," d'Artagnan said. "My need is pressing and I must have your papers."

"Lubin!" the man shouted to his servant. "Give me my pistols."

"Planchet," d'Artagnan said, "take care of the servant and I will take care of the master."

The dusty gentleman drew his sword and rushed at d'Artagnan, but he was no match for the young swordsman.

At each sword thrust, d'Artagnan called out, "For Athos, for Porthos, and for Aramis."

Finally the man collapsed and d'Artagnan bent over him to retrieve the papers. But the man thrust his sword into d'Artagnan's chest. "And one for you!" he gasped.

"And one more for me," d'Artagnan said, answering the thrust with one of his own. At this, the man lost consciousness and d'Artagnan relieved him of the papers, which showed him to be the Count de Wardes.

"Time to sail," d'Artagnan called to Planchet, who had subdued the servant.

"But you are injured," Planchet said.

"It does not feel serious," d'Artagnan said as the two hurried to the harbor master's house and then to the ship. They sailed immediately.

D'Artagnan lay down on the deck to sleep away most of the voyage. Once they docked in Dover, d'Artagnan and Planchet rented horses and rode to the capital. They found the Duke of Buckingham at the king's castle.

At seeing d'Artagnan, the duke paled. "Has anything happened to the queen?"

"I don't think so," d'Artagnan said as he handed over the letter. "But I believe she has need of your help."

The duke opened the letter and gasped to find a bloody hole in it.

"I apologize," d'Artagnan said. "I carried it close to my chest and it must have been damaged by the duel I fought with Count de Wardes. Is it damaged?"

The duke shook his head as he read. Then he said, "Come with me."

They rode to the duke's mansion. In his chambers, the duke opened a small rosewood box and drew out a diamond-studded ribbon.

He said, "If she needs them, I will be content with the box that once held them."

As he handed over the ribbon, he gasped. Even d'Artagnan could see the ragged end where the ribbon had been cut. "Two of the diamonds are missing," the duke said.

"It must be a trick of the cardinal," d'Artagnan said. "The queen is undone."

"Not yet." The duke called for the finest jeweler in London and set him to reproducing the missing diamond studs. "They must be fashioned within the next two days."

The two new studs were such a perfect match even an expert could not tell them from the originals. The duke said to d'Artagnan, "How can I reward you?"

"I need no reward from you," d'Artagnan said. "Though I am grateful for what you have done to save my queen, you are not a friend to France. I will take no gift from the king's enemy."

"Let me then give you the horses you will need to return to Paris," the duke said.

"That I can accept."

D'Artagnan traveled swiftly to catch the ship home. As he passed other ships at the dock, he caught sight of a beautiful woman. He was certain it was the woman called, "Milady." But he had no time to spend pondering it as he rushed back to Paris and to his queen.

# CHAPTER 10

# The Ball

In Paris, everyone talked about the upcoming ball. Such social parties were rare enough to be on everyone's lips. The city hall buzzed with workers transforming it for the event.

Guests began arriving at six. Arrivals were carefully timed so that the most prestigious ladies arrived fashionably late. The wife of the president of Parliament arrived at nine, as she was the second-most important lady in Paris.

No one expected the royals before midnight, and cheers rang out to announce the coming of the king. Whispers passed through the crowd about how sad the king seemed.

A half hour later, more cheers arose and the queen came into the ballroom. Like the king, she looked sad and tired. The cardinal saw her and a vicious smile crossed his face.

Finally the king stepped close to the queen to whisper fiercely, "Where are the diamonds I asked you to wear?"

"This is such a great crowd," the queen whispered back. "I feared losing them."

"You were wrong not to do as I asked." The king's face grew thunderous.

"I will have them brought to me at once," the queen promised. "I do not wish to spoil the party." She bowed to the king and slipped off to her dressing room with her ladies-in-waiting.

The cardinal crept up to the king's side and handed him a box. The king opened it to find two diamond studs.

"If the queen returns with diamonds," the cardinal said, "you will see she is missing two. Ask her where they are. Then we should talk."

The king gave him a long look and would have questioned him, but a cry of admiration came from the crowd and the king knew the queen had returned. She wore a pearl-gray coat fastened with diamond clasps and a blue satin skirt embroidered in silver. On her left shoulder a bow of a matching blue was studded with the diamonds the king had requested.

She was wearing the diamonds, but how many of them? The king could not tell from a distance, so he walked to her side and handed her the small box.

"Thank you," he said. "I believe two of your diamonds are missing and I've brought them to you."

The queen smiled brightly. "Two more, Sire? Now I have fourteen."

The king counted the twelve diamonds in the bow, then turned to the cardinal. "What does this mean, Your Eminence?"

"I wanted to give Her Majesty a gift," the cardinal said smoothly. "But I had not the daring to give them myself."

"I am sure these two cost you as much as the twelve others cost His Majesty," the queen said.

She bowed to the king and the cardinal and slipped away to her dressing room again.

In the far corner of the room, a young man watched the scene with interest. D'Artagnan was glad to see his king and queen looking happy again. He felt it wise not to be seen by the cardinal, so he turned to leave the ball.

A young woman beckoned to him from the shadows. D'Artagnan recognized Constance Bonacieux at once. She held a finger to her lips when he tried to speak, then led him through corridors and into a room with a far door covered by a thick tapestry.

Suddenly a shapely hand and arm came through an opening in the tapestry. D'Artagnan realized it was the queen, offering her hand in thanks. He fell to his knees and kissed the hand. Then it withdrew, leaving him with a ring. He heard the door close behind the tapestry and knew this audience with the queen was over.

D'Artagnan slipped the ring on his own finger and admired it. It was his first token of

thanks from a grand lady and was surely finer than anything any of the Musketeers had.

Madame Bonacieux returned to lead him back out of the maze of corridors. When he opened his mouth to speak again, she put her hand over it.

"Quiet," she whispered. "You must go now."

"When will I see you again?"

"A note waits for you at home," she answered and gave him a push toward the hall.

D'Artagnan ran all the way home and found the promised note on a table. It was an invitation to meet Constance the following night. Finally d'Artagnan felt like the grand Musketeers with their secret meetings with beautiful lady friends.

With this he thought of his dear friends. Had they returned to Paris? Had they survived their ordeal along the road? D'Artagnan tucked his letter into his cloak and headed quickly to see Monsieur de Treville.

The captain of the Musketeers was in a cheerful mood. He had seen the transformation in the king, the queen, and the cardinal.

"I know you played a part in that," Treville said. "And I see you have the ring to prove it. But beware."

"What have I to fear?" d'Artagnan asked. "I am a friend to Her Majesty."

"And an enemy to His Eminence," Treville said. "I would sell the ring and not show off your part in this event."

"Thank you for your advice. I will consider it," d'Artagnan said, though he had already made up his mind to keep the ring. "Have Athos, Porthos, and Aramis returned to Paris?"

"They have not," Treville said. "Do you know where they are?"

"I know where I left them," d'Artagnan said. He described the circumstances that had stopped each of the Musketeers. "I barely made it myself as I was wounded by Count de Wardes in Calais."

"Ah, the count is one of the cardinal's men," Treville said. "I think it would be better for your health to leave Paris for a bit. Go and find your friends."

"I have a meeting I must not miss," d'Artagnan said. "I will leave right after."

"Then travel carefully," Treville said. "And be wise in whom you trust."

# CHAPTER
## 11

# The Return

At the appointed hour, d'Artagnan arrived at the bungalow described in his note from Constance. The small house was dark and quiet. He spotted a thin ray of light shining from between the shutters on the second floor. That must be where Constance waited.

A tree grew up beside the house. D'Artagnan climbed the tree easily and scooted along a thick branch to open the shutters and peer into the second-floor window.

The door to the room hung askew from its hinges. A table filled with elegant dishes lay overturned with broken bottles and crushed fruit scattered around. Clearly someone had abducted Constance.

D'Artagnan climbed down from the tree and searched the grounds. A small hut lay in the shadows near the wall. D'Artagnan pounded on the door. An old man opened it and peered out fearfully. "Don't ask me anything, sir."

"Tell me what you know," d'Artagnan begged. "I promise I will tell no one about you."

The old man described a carriage and riders who had come to the bungalow some hours earlier. "I heard a scream and three men dragged a woman from the house."

D'Artagnan said, "Tell me about the men you saw."

"I only saw two of them clearly. One was tall and dark with a thin face and a black mustache. And one of the men was short and fat."

D'Artagnan frowned fiercely. It sounded like the scarred nobleman. Disheartened, d'Artagnan turned away. He had no idea where to begin the search for Constance. The only thing left for him to do was find his friends. If they lived, perhaps they could help.

D'Artagnan passed the night in an inn near the bungalow and then returned home to search for Athos, Porthos, and Aramis. He learned that the horses given to him by the duke had arrived, so he took them along.

He quickly made his way to Chantilly, where Porthos had stayed behind to duel. "When I was here last, I had to leave a friend behind," d'Artagnan said to the innkeeper. "Can you tell me what happened to him?"

"He has done us the honor of staying with us," the innkeeper said. "He seems to have run out of funds and when I presented him with a bill, he offered to cut off my ears."

"But he is well?" d'Artagnan asked.

"He was badly wounded," the innkeeper said. "He is much better now."

"Can I see him?"

"Certainly," the innkeeper said eagerly. "And perhaps you could take him with you?"

D'Artagnan ran up the steps to the second floor and found the tall Musketeer in bed. His servant knelt close by, cooking rabbits over a spit on the fire.

"D'Artagnan!" Porthos's face lit up at the sight of his friend. "Join us for a meal. The wretched innkeeper won't serve us, but I can count on Mousqueton to find a good meal." The servant nodded politely at the mention of his name.

D'Artagnan told his friend of everything that had happened after they parted company. "I have brought you a fine new horse to ride as soon as you are well," d'Artagnan said. "You can sell your old horse. In the meanwhile, I must see what became of our other friends."

Soon d'Artagnan rode off leaving behind one of the fine English horses. He found the inn where he had left Aramis and quickly sought out the hostess. She smiled as soon as he asked about Aramis.

"A handsome young man," she said, "wounded in the side?"

"Exactly."

"He is in room five on the third floor," she said. "But he is in the company of churchmen. One is the superior of the Jesuits. Your friend is taking holy orders."

"Oh," d'Artagnan said, then rushed to the staircase. He found Aramis seated at a long table covered with scrolls. Two older men sat on either side.

"D'Artagnan!" Aramis cried. "I am happy to see you safe. I would like to hear your opinion on what subject I should use for my thesis."

"Thesis?" d'Artagnan asked.

Aramis gestured at the piles of scrolls. "I must have a thesis before I can be ordained."

"So you have to leave behind the Musketeers . . . all of your friends," d'Artagnan said the last with particular emphasis so Aramis would know he included lady friends in his suggestion.

"Some of my friends have left me first and never even write," Aramis said sadly, then turned to the two clergymen. "I will meet with you again tomorrow."

"Good-bye till tomorrow, my son," one of the men said solemnly and they all filed out.

"You may not be as forgotten as you think." D'Artagnan grinned as he pulled a letter from his cloak. "I stopped by your house before I left Paris and found this letter for you." He sniffed it before handing it over. "It smells so sweet."

Aramis tore open the letter and read it quickly. "Oh, my friend did not leave Paris of her own choosing," he said. "She was exiled by the king. She is still my friend." Then the young Musketeer blushed having said so much.

"Do you still think it is time to enter the priesthood?" d'Artagnan asked.

Aramis laughed. "Perhaps next year."

D'Artagnan told his friend everything that had happened since last they met and showed Aramis the beautiful horse he had brought for him. Aramis mounted the horse lightly but his face quickly grew pale.

"My wound is not quite as healed as I hoped," he said. "Perhaps I should wait a few more days."

D'Artagnan agreed and promised to return as soon as he had learned what happened to Athos. "Rest," he said, "and don't join the priesthood while I am gone."

"Have no fear," Aramis said, patting his pocket. "I am happier as a Musketeer for now."

So d'Artagnan turned again to the road.

# English and French

As happy as d'Artagnan was to find Porthos and Aramis, he worried most for Athos. "If he is hurt," d'Artagnan muttered as he rode, "the innkeeper will not live to enjoy another day."

He leaped from his horse at the door of the inn, fully ready to attack. He strode through the door with his hat down low on his forehead and his hand on his sword.

"Do you recognize me?" he asked the innkeeper.

"I do not believe so," the innkeeper said, smiling.

"I will refresh your memory," d'Artagnan said. "I was here with a friend two weeks ago and you accused us of being counterfeiters."

The innkeeper turned pale. "I have regretted that every day since," he moaned. The man then told d'Artagnan how guards had come to the inn ahead of Athos and d'Artagnan. "They said a counterfeiter was coming. They said the Musketeer uniforms were only disguises!"

"A lie!" d'Artagnan boomed.

The innkeeper described how Athos had defended himself against a host of men, until he could retreat to the cellars of the inn. He locked himself inside and eventually the men left. But Athos still refused to come out!

"The cellars are where I keep all my food and drink," the innkeeper said. "When I tell him that no one means him harm, he only bellows at me through the door. If you can take your friend with you, I will be grateful."

D'Artagnan grinned at the thought of Athos eating the innkeeper out of business. The innkeeper led him to the cellar door and d'Artagnan yelled, "I am here, my friend! Will you please open the door?"

"Certainly," Athos said. The door swung open and the Musketeer's pale, grinning face appeared. D'Artagnan led Athos to the best room in the inn while the innkeeper and his wife rushed into the cellars, moaning over the bones of half-eaten hams.

D'Artagnan quickly brought Athos up to date on the health of their friends and the court intrigues he had missed.

"Now," d'Artagnan said, "my dear Constance is missing and I have no way to find her."

Athos sniffed. "You are better off without love. Let me tell you a love story. This happened to a friend of mine in my native province. He was a nobleman and a fine fellow. He fell in love with a poor young woman of exceptional beauty and married her."

"That sounds like a grand love story," d'Artagnan said.

"But she was none of the things he thought she was," Athos snarled. "Once, when they were riding, she fell from her horse and her clothes were torn. My foolish friend rushed to help her and that's when he saw it."

"What?"

"A fleur-de-lis. The tiny brand that marked her as condemned to die," Athos said.

"What did he do?" d'Artagnan asked.

"He fulfilled her sentence," Athos said. "He killed her. And that cured me of any interest in beautiful women. You should be cured, too."

The next day Athos suggested selling the English horses d'Artagnan had brought. "The English are no friends of ours," he said. "Not with war so close."

They sold the horses, bought others, and rode back to collect their friends. To d'Artagnan's surprise, each of the men had the same thought. They found Aramis and Porthos ready to return to Paris with jingling bags of money and plain French horses.

When they arrived in Paris, Monsieur de Treville notified the Musketeers that they must begin preparing their equipment to ride into war with the king by the first of May.

D'Artagnan was also preparing for the war, but he found his mind turned again and again to Constance. He knew the cardinal had played a part in her disappearance, but he couldn't confront the most powerful man in France.

Then fate seemed to smile upon him, offering an opportunity. Whenever d'Artagnan had a free moment, he would walk through the streets, hoping to find some clue to the lady's abductors. One night, he spotted a fine carriage stopped on the side of the road. A richly dressed gentleman had stopped his horse beside it. D'Artagnan could tell he was arguing with a woman inside.

D'Artagnan hurried to the carriage and doffed his hat. "This gentleman seems to have made you angry, Madame. Can I discourage him for you?"

The woman turned to look at d'Artagnan and they exchanged a surprised glance. It was the woman d'Artagnan knew as Milady. He was certain she was a spy and he wondered if she might be his key to finding Constance.

Milady laughed. "Thank you, sir, but the gentleman is my brother-in-law, Lord de Winter."

"Why is this idiot meddling in our affairs?" the gentleman demanded.

The insult drove all plans from the young man's mind. "Idiot!" he gasped, drawing his sword. "You are an idiot and an Englishman."

D'Artagnan and Lord de Winter began to duel. D'Artagnan noticed the attentive eye Milady paid to the fight. The young man limited himself to defensive moves until de Winter began to tire. Then he disarmed him with a quick flick.

Lord de Winter stepped back several steps, but his foot slipped and he fell on his back. D'Artagnan leaped toward him and put his sword to the older man's throat.

"I could kill you sir," he said. "But I'll spare you for the sake of your sister-in-law."

D'Artagnan looked sharply toward the carriage and caught a glance of disappointment and anger on the lady's face before she quickly donned a smile.

Lord de Winter was happy to put the duel behind them and embraced d'Artagnan as friend. He called out to the carriage, "You must take this young man into your good graces." "She's not without influence," he whispered to d'Artagnan.

"I'm sure that is true," d'Artagnan murmured.

"What you did today has given you a right to my lifelong gratitude," the beautiful woman said through the carriage window. "I hope you will come and see me often."

D'Artagnan assured her that he would as he bowed and smiled, already certain to be one step closer to finding Constance.

# Milady's Secret

D'Artagnan became a regular visitor to Lady de Winter's home. The beautiful woman received him graciously. And each time, the pretty maid, Kitty, blushed and smiled with every word he said to her.

Lady de Winter's attention toward him slowly pulled d'Artagnan's mind away from his beloved Constance. He knew Milady was dangerous and worked for the cardinal, but he could not help himself. She sighed often as if a deep problem pressed itself against her.

"What makes you sigh, dear lady?" d'Artagnan asked.

"Nothing." The beautiful lady looked away, blinking rapidly as if to chase away tears. "It's just that my brother-in-law pressures me so."

D'Artagnan begged for details but she waved them away. "We should not talk of sad things," she said, smiling bravely. "Tell me an amusing story of you and your friends."

And so another visit passed. D'Artagnan was falling under her spell with the certainty of a trembling rabbit staring into the hypnotic eyes of the cobra. As he left the lady's chamber, the young maid led him aside.

"I need to talk to you, sir," she said hesitantly. "You are in love with my mistress?"

"Yes," d'Artagnan admitted. "Madly in love."

"That's a pity. She doesn't love you at all."

D'Artagnan frowned. "And you have proof?"

"I can give you proof," Kitty said. "Instead of visiting my mistress tomorrow, come to the back door near midnight. I will secret you in here. This room opens into my mistress's bedroom. From here, you will hear my lady say how she really feels."

D'Artagnan looked at the young maid's honest face and agreed. He fretted throughout the next day, barely able to concentrate on anything but the coming discovery. In his heart, he knew what he would learn but clung to hope that the young maid was mistaken.

Late into the night, he crept around Milady's house to find Kitty waiting in the shadows. She led him to the room again. There she kissed his cheek, then hurried into Lady de Winter's room when they both heard the woman call.

"I can't believe d'Artagnan did not call at all this evening," Lady de Winter fretted as Kitty helped her change for bed.

"You miss him," Kitty murmured. "You must love him very much."

The other woman laughed at that. "Love him? I despise him. But he will be useful to me. Already the silly boy adores me. I will send him to England to kill both my tiresome brother-in-law and the cardinal's enemy."

"The cardinal's enemy?" Kitty echoed.

"The Duke of Buckingham," Lady de Winter said. "The cardinal is angry with me because d'Artagnan thwarted our last plan. How fitting it will be if the silly child kills the duke himself."

"That sounds dangerous," Kitty whispered.

"Yes," the other woman laughed again. "And if d'Artagnan is killed during the assassination, all the better. It will save my having to find another fool to kill him later."

At this d'Artagnan could take no more. He burst into Lady de Winter's room and shouted. "I am not such a fool as you think!"

Milady shrieked with fury and grabbed a slender knife from her bedside. She rushed at d'Artagnan with the knife raised. They wrestled over the knife and d'Artagnan pulled it from her grasp, knocking her to the floor.

When she fell, her gown dropped from her shoulder and d'Artagnan stared in horror. She wore the fleur-de-lis brand that Athos had described so clearly.

D'Artagnan gasped. "The brand!"

Lady de Winter clasped a hand over her shoulder and began shrieking for guards, servants, someone to save her from attack. At that, d'Artagnan turned and fled through the empty room and down the stairs to the outside. He ran with all his strength to the home of Athos, knowing he must tell his friend what he had seen.

He burst into his friend's room to find Porthos and Aramis there as well. "Ah, d'Artagnan is joining us," Porthos cried. "We thought we had lost you to romance."

Athos immediately saw how pale d'Artagnan was. "What is wrong?"

"Treason," the young man gasped. "Plots, the brand, we must do something!"

"Calm down," Aramis urged. "That made no sense at all!"

But Athos had caught the word *brand* and led his young friend to a chair to sit. "Tell us what you know," he urged. "As soon as you have caught your breath."

# A Terrible Vision

When d'Artagnan could speak normally, he told his friend of the plot against Lady De Winter's brother-in-law and the Duke of Buckingham.

"We must warn them," d'Artagnan said.

"Warn Englishmen?" Porthos shouted. "France would be well served by two less Englishmen. The Duke of Buckingham urges England to war. Certainly this time, we should simply step aside."

"Anything Lady de Winter wants," d'Artagnan said, "could not be for the good of England."

"I suspect it is for the good of the cardinal," Aramis said.

"And for herself," Athos added. "The more I hear of her, the more I fear she is a deadly foe." He looked directly at d'Artagnan and the young man knew he and Athos had come to the same conclusion about the brand on Milady's shoulder.

"I am not afraid, but she intended to use me as her puppet," d'Artagnan muttered. "I would spoil her plan just for that."

"It would not be easy to send a note to England," Porthos said, his boots thumping on the floor as he paced. "War looms very close. Such a note could result in our being tried for treason."

Aramis smiled slightly. "I have friends in many places."

"Lady friends?" Porthos asked, grinning.

Aramis blushed but ignored him. "I believe I can have the note reach its destination safely and we can surely write it in such a way that no one will see treason in it."

The friends huddled together and wrote the note, which Aramis sent swiftly on its way with his servant. The three then turned their conversation to keeping d'Artagnan safe.

"All of us will be leaving Paris soon," d'Artagnan said. "The guards are to leave in the next few days. And I know you will be leaving soon after with the king. Surely, we will be uninteresting to the cardinal after that."

The friends nodded. D'Artagnan had a good point. They must only survive the next few days. Before he left for home, D'Artagnan begged Aramis to ask among his many friends for word of Constance.

"Now that I have made such an enemy of Lady de Winter, I worry for Constance."

"I will ask," Aramis said. "And when I know, I will tell you."

D'Artagnan walked through the streets of Paris as dawn broke. When he reached his rooms, he found a number of the Cardinal's Guards waiting for him.

"You will come with us," the leader of the guards announced.

Exhausted, the young man knew he would not win against so many. He followed quietly, expecting to be thrown in prison immediately. He was shocked when the guards led him to the rooms of the cardinal himself!

"Are you one of the d'Artagnan's of Bearn?" the thin-faced older man asked.

"Yes, Monseigneur," d'Artagnan replied.

"Many things have happened to you since you came to Paris," the cardinal said quietly.

"Have I displeased you, Your Eminence?" the young man asked.

"You have followed orders with exceptional courage and intelligence. I do not punish men for being loyal and doing a job well," the cardinal said. "I have plans for you."

D'Artagnan suppressed a shudder at the thought of the cardinal's plans.

"You are brave and careful," the cardinal said. "But you have strong enemies that may crush you. I have prevented this in small ways so far, but I would like my protection over you to be visible. I wish to offer you a place as a lieutenant in the Cardinal's Guards."

D'Artagnan stared at the older man in disbelief. He had expected to be thrown in prison and instead he could be made an officer? The young man cleared his throat gently and said, "I am in His Majesty's Guards and have no reason to regret it. I hope some day to be a Musketeer with my dearest friends."

"In other words, you refuse to serve me," the cardinal said. When d'Artagnan leaned forward to protest, the older man held up a hand. "I don't hold it against you. Loyalty is a wonderful thing, but understand the danger you will be under without my clear protection."

"I will remember both your kind offer and your wise advice," d'Artagnan said.

The cardinal dismissed him and the young man hurried home to prepare to leave with the

guards. He did not see the cardinal's next guest. If he had, he would have been truly afraid, for Lady de Winter joined the cardinal.

"You plan to kill Buckingham yourself?" the cardinal asked.

"No, I cannot move against him directly," Milady said. "He has not trusted me since I stole the diamonds. But I will find someone who will do the job for me. England is filled with romantic young men."

"I am sure you will," the cardinal agreed. "What do you need from me?"

"I would like permission to kill Constance Bonacieux," Lady de Winter said. "She played a large part in the queen's diamond episode."

The cardinal nodded his approval so Lady de Winter continued. "And I need a paper from you stating that what I do, I do for you. If I am forced to take direct action against the duke, I will need such papers to get safely back to France."

The cardinal wrote out the note she requested and handed it over. Then Lady de Winter left for England.

# Officer

Lady de Winter found a surprise awaiting her when she reached England. Soldiers waited at the boat dock and took her into custody. They loaded her in a carriage and drove furiously through London and out of the city. Not one of the soldiers would speak to the lady, no matter how charming she tried to be.

Finally, they reached a gravel drive to a massive, grim castle. She was led to a small room and locked in. She paced the floor, wondering what had happened.

Finally the door opened and Lady de Winter was shocked to see her brother-in-law stride in. He was followed by a young soldier.

"I have received letters from someone I trust. I learned you were coming to England to see me and to see the Duke of Buckingham," Lord de Winter said. "But I understand neither of us was to survive your visit."

"How could you believe such horrible things?" she asked. "We are family!"

"Yes, we are," the older man said. "Ever since your marriage to my dear brother. It's so sad he died shockingly soon after the wedding."

"Surely you don't blame me for that!" she demanded.

"I have come to believe you are capable of anything," Lord de Winter said. "And so you will stay here until the time comes to load you aboard a ship for the colonies. You will be banished from England."

Lady de Winter glared at him. She had no interest in living the rough life of a colonist. And she would succeed in her mission.

"Lieutenant Fenton will oversee your care in the days you are here," her brother-in-law said, gesturing to the young man standing straight and silent beside him. "He knows what a monster you are so you need not trouble yourself with tricks. You will be here until it is time for you to be exiled."

At that, the two men left and Lady de Winter raged around the room, flinging things and fuming. Then she stopped. The lieutenant her brother-in-law had left to guard her was very young and very solemn. She might find her escape yet.

Lady de Winter settled quietly in a chair and pondered what she had observed of the young man. He was nothing like d'Artagnan and would fall for flattery and flirting.

As she planned her next move, she heard firm footsteps in the hall. She dropped to her knees on the floor and bowed her head. The door creaked open and she heard the young officer as she raised her head.

"Excuse me," he said. "I did not mean to interrupt your prayers."

"Please do not mock my prayers," she said, slowly rising to her feet. "I can handle my brother-in-law's cruel lies but I will not have my God mocked."

The young man blinked at her. "I was not mocking you," he said quietly. "I am a man of faith myself. I would not make fun of prayer." He held out a tray. "I brought your dinner."

Lady de Winter had to force herself not to smile in triumph. She had surely found her opening. "I do not eat such rich food," she said. "Those are the delights of my brother-in-law. I prefer simple bread, vegetables, and water."

"As do I," the young man agreed.

Lady de Winter settled down to a long talk about her imaginary religious life with the earnest young man. She continued the talks any time the young soldier came alone to her room. With each visit, she knew the young soldier cared for her more and more.

Lady de Winter knew she didn't have much time. She needed the young lieutenant to set her free from the castle but she needed much more. Her job in England would not be complete until the Duke of Buckingham was assassinated. She could not return to France having failed the cardinal again.

When she was alone, she plotted ways to make the young lieutenant hate the duke. She knew most citizens did not like Buckingham, but it was the religious who hated him most for wild living. Suddenly Lady de Winter knew how to lure her young lieutenant into solving all her problems.

"Could I ask a simple thing of you?" she asked the man when he delivered her dinner.

He looked away, clearly upset. "I cannot help you escape."

"I would not ask that," she assured him. "I am afraid." She paused, dropping her eyes. "If the Duke of Buckingham comes here. Will you tell me and will you . . . bring me a knife?"

The young lieutenant's eyes widened. "You would attack the duke?"

Lady de Winter laughed bitterly. "I only wish my plan were so simple. No, I . . . I cannot face him forcing himself on me. Not again. I would rather die. If he comes to be with me before I am sent into exile, will you bring me a knife that I can die with some small honor left?"

"What do you mean if he forces himself on you again?" the man asked, his cheeks flushed.

"Oh, please, do not ask me to speak of my shame," Lady de Winter said. "I was young and he was powerful. What could I do when he . . . when he hurt me." She dropped her voice to a sob.

"He hurt you?" the lieutenant roared.

"He likes to hurt young women who have a deep faith," she said softly. "He finds it funny to destroy our honor."

By the young man's trembling fury, Lady de Winter knew she had won. He would kill Buckingham for her and surely he would save her as well. Now she had only to guide him to his own destruction and her victory.

# The Convent

When word of the assassination of the Duke of Buckingham reached France, the king and the cardinal rejoiced. Both knew Buckingham had hoped to capture France and end up with the French queen as his own wife. With his death, the English king had little interest in war.

The small battles within France to clear out English sympathizers had gone well. The Musketeers found they now had time to spend with their young friend d'Artagnan again.

"I cannot say I weep for Buckingham," Porthos said.

"I see the hand of Lady de Winter in this," d'Artagnan insisted. "And any success for her cannot be good."

"Well, if she is in England, all the better for you," Porthos said. "She would have trouble plunging a knife into your heart from there."

D'Artagnan merely slumped gloomily. His feeling of impending doom had grown stronger with the news of the duke's death. Lady de Winter's victory would surely give her the power of the cardinal behind her revenge.

"At least Lord de Winter is well," Aramis said gently. "And I have still better news."

"Please, Aramis," d'Artagnan said. "Tell me."

"I have found Constance Bonacieux."

"In prison?" d'Artagnan asked.

Aramis shook his head. "In a convent in Bethune. The queen had her taken from prison and has hidden her at the convent."

D'Artagnan leaped to his feet. "I must go there at once."

"Why?" Porthos asked. "She is surely safe."

Finally Athos spoke. "No, I am certain she will be Lady de Winter's next target and if Aramis's friend could find her, so could her enemies. We should ride at once." And so the friends leaped to their horses.

What the friends did not know was that Lady de Winter was well ahead of them. The young lieutenant had kindly broken her out of her brother-in-law's castle and brought her to a ship heading for France. Then he had ridden to London to kill the duke and die for his treason.

As soon as Lady de Winter reached Paris, she had received her reward—the location of Constance Bonacieux. While the Musketeers and d'Artagnan mounted their horses outside the inn, Lady de Winter was already at the convent becoming friends with her next victim.

Lady de Winter sat in a small tower room with Constance. "My friends in Paris have told me you are not safe," she said to Constance. "The cardinal is sending men after you."

Constance looked at her new friend in alarm. "What can I do? Oh, if only d'Artagnan was here. He would save me."

"I am sure he would," Lady de Winter replied. "But I can take you to a safe place where the cardinal's men cannot find you. First, we eat so we will be strong for the trip."

"Oh yes, good idea," Constance said. "I'm so lucky you came."

"Do doubt," Lady de Winter said, filling Constance's glass. "Here now, eat and drink."

Constance drank deeply as Lady de Winter's smile widened. Suddenly, both women heard the pounding of hoofbeats.

"Is it the cardinal's men?" Constance cried.

"I will look." Lady de Winter peered out the window as the horsemen rode into view. She recognized the uniforms and plumed hats of the Musketeers. She saw d'Artagnan in the lead.

"Too late," she whispered. "You are too late."

"It is the cardinal's men," she said, turning to face Constance.

"Oh no!" Constance jumped up from the table and crumpled to the floor. "I am too weak. You must flee without me."

Lady de Winter ran out of the room. Constance sat on the floor as waves of dizziness passed over her. She heard the pounding of footsteps on the tower stairs and turned weakly toward the door.

D'Artagnan rushed in and dropped to his knees beside her, wrapping his arms around her.

"Oh, d'Artagnan," Constance whispered. "I am so glad to see you, but I feel so strange. So cold." She shuddered in d'Artagnan's arms. "I was afraid you were the cardinal's men. My friend must have been mistaken."

"What friend?" d'Artagnan asked.

"Lady de Winter," Constance said, her voice thinner. "She has been so kind." Her face grew ashen and she gasped for breath.

As the last breaths of life passed from her lips, d'Artagnan held her closer. Finally, d'Artagnan lay Constance gently down. More footsteps sounded on the stairs and Lord de Winter entered.

He took one look and said, "I fear I am too late. My sister-in-law has been here before me."

"She has," d'Artagnan said. "But this is the last evil thing she will do."

"You track her," Athos told his friends. "I must collect someone. I will follow as close behind you as I can."

At that, the friends parted. D'Artagnan led the way outside. They found slipper prints where Lady de Winter had run through the gardens behind the convent. The abbess of the convent followed them to the edge of the property, where they found signs of a carriage.

"She must have planned her escape for some time," Porthos said. "I do not know how long we can track a carriage."

"I may have an idea where she went," the abbess said. "She had only one visitor while she was here. A tall man with a thin scar on his face. She said he was her brother." She paused as Lord de Winter snorted at this remark. "She told him to meet her at Armentières."

"And so we ride," d'Artagnan said. "To Armentières." He turned to Lord de Winter. "Will you wait and tell Athos where we go?"

The other man nodded. "We will meet you there."

The men rode away in silence, each with dark thoughts of revenge. They rode without pause to Armentières. There they learned a beautiful young woman had rented a small house on the riverbank. They turned toward the house just as more riders joined them. Athos and Lord de Winter had caught up, along with a stranger. No one asked Athos about the extra man. Instead they simply turned grimly toward the small house.

Athos broke open the door to the house. Lady de Winter took one look at his pale, fierce face and shrieked, "Why are you here?"

"I have come to finish what I started years ago," Athos replied. "I am here to serve a sentence of death upon the Countess de La Fere . . . known now as Lady de Winter."

# The Conclusion

Lady de Winter stared Athos in the face. "So you would murder me?"

"No," Athos said. "You will face the list of your crimes and then you will die by execution."

D'Artagnan stepped around his friend and pointed. "I accuse this woman of poisoning Constance Bonacieux, who died last night."

"We bear witness," his friends said together.

Lord de Winter stepped forward. "I accuse this woman of having the Duke of Buckingham murdered by corrupting a fine young soldier, who died for believing in her."

D'Artagnan shuddered as he remember how easily he had fallen under the woman's spell as well.

"I also believe she killed my brother," Lord de Winter said. "He died within three hours of marrying her from a strange illness that choked the life from him."

"Like Constance," d'Artagnan said softly.

Athos stepped forward then. "And I accuse this woman of bearing the fleur-de-lis brand of the condemned on her shoulder. I know she wears it, as she was my wife."

Milady leaped to her feet. "I defy you to name one person who can say what crime you claim I must have committed."

"Silence," called a voice no one recognized. "That is for me to answer."

All eyes turned to the man with Athos. The man walked up to Lady de Winter and threw back the hood that hid his face.

"Oh no!" she screamed. "It can't be. You're a ghost. Help! The executioner of Lille!"

"I can tell the story of this woman. She was a young nun in a Benedictine convent. She lured a young priest into robbing the church and running away with her. She and the priest were captured and I branded them for execution. The priest killed himself out of shame, but she convinced a jailer to help her escape. Tonight, I will complete her sentence. I do it for justice and for my brother, the young priest."

"No, you cannot!" she shrieked. "I have a pardon from the cardinal himself." She pulled the paper from her gown and Lord de Winter snatched if from her.

"I am not bound by rules of a French cardinal," he said. "Tonight you will pay for your crimes."

It was nearly midnight when Lady de Winter was led from the small building. The witnesses stood at a distance as the executioner brought her to a small rock overlooking the water. And the executioner completed the sentence passed against her so many years before.

When the friends returned to Paris, d'Artagnan found another summons from the cardinal waiting for him.

"We will go together," Porthos thundered. "If he throws you in prison, we will break you out!"

D'Artagnan smiled at his friend's courage. "That might be extreme."

"But it might be wise," Athos said, "to show you are not without friends."

"Good idea," Porthos said. "I will round up a few more friends."

So d'Artagnan went quickly to the audience with the cardinal. Before he left, Athos slipped a paper into d'Artagnan's cloak. "You never know what might help," he said.

When d'Artagnan arrived, the cardinal looked at him gravely. "You have been accused of a number of crimes, including treason."

"And who accuses me?" d'Artagnan asked. "A woman branded by French justice? A woman who poisons the innocent?"

"If she has committed the crimes you say, she will be punished," the cardinal said.

"She has already been punished," d'Artagnan said. "She is dead."

"You admit to murder?" the cardinal asked.

"I did, but I believe I have your pardon." D'Artagnan drew out the document Athos had given him and lay it before the cardinal. The cardinal opened it and recognized his own handwriting absolving the bearer of any punishment. The older man stared at the paper for a long time and finally looked up.

"This makes things much easier," he said. He stood and crossed the room to write out a new document. "Here, I give you this in exchange for the document you have given me."

D'Artagnan looked down at the paper. It was a lieutenant's commission in the Musketeers. The young man's knees buckled and he was forced to sit.

"You're a fine boy, d'Artagnan," the cardinal said. "Whether you serve in my guards or the Musketeers, I know you will serve France. My heart is French, and there is nothing I want more than what is good for France."

"I'll never forget, Monseigneur," d'Artagnan said.

At that moment, another man walked into the room. He was tall with a thin scar on his face.

"You!" d'Artagnan said, leaping to his feet with his hand on his sword.

"Enough," the cardinal said. "Rochefort is my trusted friend." He turned to the scarred man. "I now count d'Artagnan as my friend as well. Whatever had been between you in the past is no more. Is that understood?"

Both men nodded and the cardinal dismissed them. D'Artagnan left with his mind in a muddle. He walked out onto the street. A crowd of Musketeers cheered. Porthos had brought everyone he knew to defend his friend.

Tears rolled down d'Artagnan's cheeks as he recognized how much he had to be grateful for. He told his friend of his new commission and they celebrated with him long into the night.